Fiona Simmonite
6 Spottiswoode Gardens
St Andrews
Fife Scotland
Phone 7533
Thankyou

Contents

SBN 361 04413 5
Copyright © 1979 Martspress Ltd.
Published in 1979 by Purnell Books Ltd.,
Berkshire House, Queen Street, Maidenhead, Berkshire
Made and printed in Great Britain by Purnell and Sons Limited
Paulton (Bristol) and London

To Fiona
from
Gillian
xxxx

THE PURNELL BOOK OF
Famous
Fairy Stories

Stories adapted by Barbara Hayes
Illustrations by Ronald S. Embleton

Snow White

Long ago and far away, in the days when witches and fairies roamed the earth and the countryside was covered in thick dark forests, there lived a king and a queen and a princess.

The king was rich and the queen was beautiful and the princess was good and lovely and one might have thought that all three would have been happy and contented—but they were not.

You see, the queen was the king's second wife. She was not the mother of the lovely little princess, and the more the king loved his daughter, the princess, the more the queen *hated* her.

The queen was jealous.

If the princess practised playing the harp, the queen would snap: "Can't that wretched girl ever be quiet? My head is splitting with the noise of that terrible twanging. How she can call it music I don't know!"

And if the princess played with one of the royal dogs, the queen would order her to turn the dog out into the yard, where it belonged, or so the queen said.

The queen was jealous even if the dog loved the princess.

Of course all this bad temper upset the king and, for the sake of keeping peace with the queen, he tried not to show too much love for Snow White.

Snow White! That was the name of the lovely little princess.

What a very unusual name that was!

It had been a very bitter winter, the year Snow White had been born and as her mother, the first queen, had been sewing baby clothes, she had accidentally pricked her finger and a drop of blood had fallen on to the white snow.

"That is how I should like my baby to be," smiled the queen, "with a skin as white as the snow, lips as red as blood and hair as black as the ebony wood of this window sill."

So as those were magical times and as the queen was a very important lady, her wish was granted and when her baby girl was born in the springtime, her skin was as white as snow, her lips as red as blood and her hair as black as ebony.

How happy the queen was.

"We will call the little girl Snow White," she smiled—and so it was.

But happy days are all too short; Snow White's mother died and the king married again. The new queen's face was beautiful, but her heart was black with evil and her eyes were green with jealousy.

In fact many things were strange about the beautiful new queen—not the least being that hidden behind a curtain in her private room she kept a talking mirror.

If the queen gazed into the secret glowing depths of the mirror, she saw not her own reflection, but a swirling, shimmering face, which spoke only the truth.

Every day the queen would gaze into the mirror and ask: "Mirror, mirror on the wall, who is the fairest one of all?"

And for years the mirror had answered: "Lovely lady, slim and tall, you are the fairest one of all."

But the day came when the mirror gave an answer which the queen did not wish to hear.

"As I hang upon this wall, Snow White is the fairest one of all," chanted the mirror.

The queen was FURIOUS.

But she knew the mirror always spoke the truth. Snow White *was* the fairest.

The queen's green eyes burned with jealous hatred. She drew the curtain across the magic mirror, walked from her

room and stared coldly at Snow White laughing happily with her father.

The love in the king's face as he smiled at Snow White sealed his pretty, young daughter's fate.

Secretly the wicked queen sent for a royal huntsman. She sat smiling at him in the rose garden, clinking a handful of thick golden coins between her fingers.

"That Snow White is a trouble-maker," said the queen. "She is turning the king against me. She must go. How grateful I should be to the man who would take Snow White deep into the forest and kill her."

The huntsman's blood chilled with horror at those wicked words, but his eyes noticed how the gold coins gleamed richly in the sunlight.

The queen turned her heartless gaze full on the shivering huntsman. "I would give this gold to the man who would bring me Snow White's heart to prove she was dead," murmured the queen, "but to a man who refused my request, I would be very —ungrateful."

The next day the huntsman took Snow White deep into the dark forest which covered the land all round the little kingdom.

How Snow White enjoyed the trip into the forest, and as the huntsman looked at her pretty, young face, he could not bring himself to kill her.

However, his feelings were not so kindly that he did not still want the gold. He told Snow White of the wicked queen's plot.

"Run away into the forest and never come back and I will tell the queen you are dead," advised the huntsman.

Snow White was terrified. She ran and

ran, trying to get as far as she could from the hatred of the wicked queen. And the huntsman slew a deer and took its heart to the queen and she thought it was the heart of Snow White.

Now the dark forest is a frightening place and Snow White gasped with joy when she saw a pretty little cottage—a *very* little cottage actually.

She knocked at the door, but no one answered. Then, as it was cold and night was falling, Snow White pushed open the door of the cottage and went inside.

There was no one at home, but the place was cosy and welcoming and the table was laid for supper for seven people.

"Perhaps I could eat a mouthful or two," thought Snow White. "I am so hungry."

So she ate a little of everything and hoped that no one would notice that some of the food was missing.

Then, tired out by all the horrid things

that had happened to her, weary Snow White stumbled across to one of the seven beds, which were also in the cottage, and fell into a deep, exhausted sleep.

How lucky for Snow White that she had found the cottage, just as dusk was falling, but she was even luckier than she knew.

The cottage belonged to seven kindly little men who would shelter Snow White in her time of danger.

However, the little men knew nothing of all this yet. They were dwarfs and they were also miners. Every day they went to dig for gold and jewels in the nearby mountains.

And every evening they trotted home thinking how nice supper was going to taste and how good it would be to have a restful evening in their cosy little cottage home.

The cottage only needed to be little, you see, because the dwarfs were such *little* folk.

But no doubt you have heard the old saying: "There is many a slip betwixt cup and lip."

And of course when the hungry dwarfs arrived home they noticed at once that someone had been nibbling at their supper. And then, as Snow White was so much bigger than they were, they couldn't help noticing that she was lying on one of the beds.

"And where have you come from, young lady?" they asked—in quite a friendly way. Snow White woke with a start.

Meanwhile, at the palace, the queen was

so sure that Snow White was dead that for days and weeks she did not bother to ask her magic mirror who was the fairest in the land, but one day, at last, she did.

"*Mirror, mirror on the wall,*
  Who is the fairest one of all?"
she smiled, quite sure that she knew the answer and that the answer would be what she wanted to hear.

But the mirror glowed brightly and truth shimmered from its depths:

"*Far away o'er fen and glen,*
Snow White dwells with little men.
And though your grace is slim and tall,
Snow White is the fairest one of all."
The queen turned away with rage burning in her wicked, black heart.

"So the huntsman lied and Snow White is alive," she murmured. Then she smiled her thin, cruel smile.

"But not for long," she added.

Now, in all those weeks when the queen

had not bothered to question her magic mirror, Snow White had been living happy and safe in the cottage belonging to the seven dwarfs. While the dwarfs worked in their mine, Snow White looked after the pretty cottage—but the dwarfs were always anxious for her safety.

"We know the queen, your stepmother, of old," they said. "She is not only wicked, but clever with it. She will try to harm you again. Be very careful of any stranger."

But it is rather dreary shut up alone doing housework all day long and when one day an old peasant woman knocked at the cottage door selling pretty combs, Snow White bought one.

What a terrible mistake—because of course the peasant woman was the queen in disguise—and the comb was— POISONED!

AAAAH! Poor Snow White.

The trusting little princess had no

sooner run the comb through her beautiful ebony black hair than the poison seized her in its grip and she fell down as if dead.

How the old peasant woman laughed.

"Well, you are no longer the fairest in the land now, Snow White," she sneered. "The magic mirror will return me a better answer when I speak to it tonight."

And off she ran, just as the seven dwarfs came trudging home from their work in the mine.

"I wonder what Snow White has cooked for our supper tonight?" the dwarfs were saying to each other. And they had just made up their minds that they hoped supper would be stew with dumplings, when they caught sight of the old peasant woman hurrying away from their cottage.

"Who is that?" they gasped. "It is no one who lives round here. It can't be. No one else *does* live round here."

Then they thought of Snow White alone in the cottage and they were afraid.

Could the peasant woman have been the queen in disguise? The dwarfs ran home dreading to think of what they would find.

And oh! Their worst fears were true!

Snow White lay on a bed as if dead. It seemed that the wicked queen had won.

"Oh, Snow White, Snow White, come back to us," sobbed the heart-broken dwarfs, shaking poor Snow White—and as

they did so, the poisoned comb fell from Snow White's ebony black hair and the poison lost its power and Snow White came back to life.

The dwarfs were so happy, but they were still scared.

"Beware of strangers," they warned. "The wicked queen will strike again."

How right the dwarfs were! The wicked queen ran home full of happiness because

Snow White was dead. "Now I am the most beautiful lady in the land," sighed the queen, happily pulling the curtain back from the magic mirror, because although the queen *knew* she was so beautiful, she still wanted to hear someone else say so.

Of course by now the queen had taken off her disguise as a peasant woman and she was again her grand and lovely self.

"Mirror, mirror on the wall,
Who is the fairest one of all?"
chanted the queen, almost singing in her happiness to think that once again she herself would be the most beautiful lady in the kingdom.

Imagine her rage and disbelief when the mirror replied:

"Lovely queen, thou art so fair,
But Snow White living o'er the fen
With the seven little men
Has a beauty far more rare."
Then the queen knew that she had failed and that Snow White still lived and she raged and stormed in her anger.

"That wretched little brat with her white face and her red lips and her black hair! Shall I never be rid of her?" screamed the queen.

But then the queen calmed down and another plot formed in her cunning brain. She sat amongst her bottles and jars and magic potions and made an apple, rosy on one side and green on the other.

The apple was so pretty and crunchy looking that no one would see it and not wish to bite it.

But the apple was POISONED.

Then once more the queen disguised herself and set off to call at the cottage belonging to the seven dwarfs.

As before, the queen waited until the dwarfs were far away working in their mine. And as before, Snow White was by herself in the lonely cottage.

Well, one might have thought that after the fright with the comb Snow White would have kept the doors barred against strangers, but young heads are thoughtless and lonely hours drag by wearily and Snow White had done the same housework so many times over that it was just no fun any more.

When the friendly old lady came knocking at the door, Snow White was glad to have someone to talk to.

"You are such a pretty little girl, I should like to give you this apple as a present," smiled the old lady, who was really the queen.

Snow White felt a little doubtful. "You are so kind and the apple is so rosy," smiled Snow White, "but I don't think I should eat it till the dwarfs get home and say that I may."

The queen was furious, but she hid her anger with a smile.

"But the apple is harmless, my dear," she whined. "Look. I will eat some myself." And she took a bite from the green side—which held no poison.

Of course, when Snow White saw the old lady eating the apple and no harm coming to her, she felt that the apple was safe and that her fears were silly.

She took the apple indoors and bit into the lovely rosy side.

Ah—poor, young, foolish Snow White. She should have remembered the dwarfs' warning.

As she tried to swallow the bite of rosy apple, it stuck in her throat and Snow White fell dead to the floor.

The wicked queen watching through the cottage window laughed with joy.

"Now I am the fairest in the land," she rejoiced.

And when she had taken off her disguise, indeed she was.

The queen returned to her royal palace and lived in happiness through the long summer days, not caring one jot for the misery she had brought to so many other people.

And the seven dwarfs trotted home from their mine not knowing that they would find their beloved Snow White dead. Or at least—so it seemed.

"Snow White! Snow White! We're home," called the dwarfs, as they trotted back as usual from the mine.

"I hope she has made that meat pie she

promised," puffed one of the dwarfs.

"And that she has made lots of *thick* gravy to go with it," added another. "I can't stand *thin* gravy."

But as they approached the cottage, the dwarfs began to feel uneasy. No nice smell of baking pie drifted across the clearing and no steam from bubbling gravy, thick or thin, curled through the kitchen window.

And worst of all, Snow White was not standing in the cottage doorway as usual,

eagerly looking for their return home.

The dwarfs ran into the cottage and saw what they knew they would see.

Snow White lay dead. She had gone away. They were left alone. Now they had only their unhappiness.

The wicked queen had won. How cruel the ways of the world did seem.

But of course all this happened way back in the days of magic and things weren't really as bad as they appeared.

To start with, although Snow White

16

neither breathed nor spoke nor moved, somehow she didn't seem to be dead.

The colour still stayed in her blood red lips and her black ebony hair stayed as glossy and beautiful as ever.

It just did not seem right to bury anything so lovely in the cold dark ground. So the dwarfs made a coffin of crystal clear glass and rested Snow White inside it where every day they could see her unfading loveliness.

The dwarfs put the coffin on the mountainside near their mine and every day they stood beside it and remembered the happy days, when Snow White had been alive.

Then one day a handsome prince came riding through the mountain passes on his fine white horse.

How surprised he was when he looked across a rocky valley and saw seven little men grouped around a crystal coffin. The prince was even more surprised when he rode closer and saw that inside the coffin was a beautiful girl with skin as white as snow, lips as red as blood and hair as black as ebony.

The prince had never seen anyone more lovely in all his life and at once he fell in love with Snow White.

How hopeless for the poor prince to love a dead girl, but remember, those were magic days.

"Please let me take the coffin back to my palace where it can rest in a fine room and be far safer than out here in all weathers on this rugged mountainside," begged the prince.

The dwarfs weren't at all pleased with that suggestion.

"We want to keep Snow White here where we can look after her," they explained.

But then they remembered that they weren't getting any younger and the day might come when they no longer had the strength to climb the steep mountainside and brush the dead leaves or the drifted snow from the crystal that sheltered their beloved Snow White.

"Fate sent the prince to help us," they decided.

And they were right.

If the prince had not clattered past on his fine horse, Snow White might have lain still on the mountainside for many a

long year, but because of the prince, the seven dwarfs picked up the crystal coffin and moved it.

"We will carry Snow White down from the mountains and take her safely to your palace," they said to the prince.

But the little chaps were in such a dither at moving the crystal coffin after so long and they were handling it so very carefully so that it would not fall that, of course, they *did* drop it.

And then—how wonderful! The bump of the coffin landing on the ground jerked the piece of rosy apple from Snow White's throat and she breathed again and sat up alive and well.

How puzzled she was to find herself out on the mountainside and to see the dwarfs looking so surprised and pleased.

"The wicked queen gave you a poisoned apple and you have lain as dead for many a long year," explained the dwarfs, "but

18

now you are alive again, dear Snow White."

Then Snow White turned her eyes to see the handsome prince and they smiled at each other and they knew that they were in love.

"Will you make me the happiest man in the world by marrying me and coming to live in my palace?" asked the prince.

"Indeed I will," replied Snow White, because although she didn't know the prince very well, she could remember that palaces were very nice places, with servants to do all the work and it had been getting rather lonely in the dwarfs' cottage, by herself all day long.

And although the dwarfs were sorry to lose Snow White again so soon, they knew it was only right that a pretty princess should marry a handsome prince, so they picked flowers for joy and went with Snow White and the prince down to his palace to join in all the wedding feasting.

"After all," Snow White explained to them, "now I am the mistress of a fine palace you will always have somewhere to stay when you need a holiday or when you are too old to work."

So the dwarfs felt very pleased and had no more worries for the rest of their lives.

"Three cheers for Snow White and her prince," they laughed.

But there was one person who was not pleased by this happy turn of events—and

I am sure you can guess who it was.

The wicked queen!

One evening, as usual, the queen gazed happily into her magic mirror and just so that she could hear yet again how beautiful she was, she asked:

"Mirror, mirror on the wall,
Who is the fairest one of all?"

How astounded she was when the mirror replied:

"Lady, lady standing there,
Than thee there is a bride more fair."

The queen was FURIOUS.

"So there is a bride more fair than I am, is there?" she hissed. "Well, as I said about Snow White, NOT FOR LONG. I will soon put this new bride out of the way, just as I did that brat of a girl."

Then the queen picked up a heavy candlestick and stepped towards the mirror.

"And I've had enough of your giving the wrong answers, too," she snapped. "There is such a thing as saying the right thing at the wrong time, you know—and you have done it once too often."

The queen smashed the mirror to pieces.

How ungrateful!

But the queen was like that.

Then the wretched jealous queen raced through the land until she found the bride about whom the mirror had spoken and, of

course, the bride was Snow White! But this time the dwarfs were ready.

They tricked the queen into putting on a pair of magic shoes which danced her into the far distance and kept the queen from ever coming near Snow White again.

So Snow White and the prince lived happily ever after.

The Golden Bird

Many years ago, when the land was divided into very small kingdoms, there was a tiny realm called Forestia.

This was because most of the realm was covered with thick forest.

Of course there were many woodcutters in Forestia and one of the strongest and most honest was a young man called Franz.

One day Franz was working hard amongst the trees, as usual, when a group of finely dressed people came riding by.

Franz had never seen such thorough-bred horses, nor such beautiful and elegant ladies and gentlemen.

And this was hardly surprising because Franz was looking at the Queen of Forestia and some of her courtiers.

The village folk with whom Franz usually mixed had neither the time nor the money to spend making themselves look so grand as the queen.

How Franz stared as the beautiful people rode past him.

"You are looking at the Queen of Forestia, young man," called one of the fine lords. "Let us see you make a bow."

So Franz bowed low before the queen and vowed that he was her loyal and hard-working subject.

His mother had always brought him up to be well mannered, you see.

The queen was very pleased with Franz's politeness and she stopped and spoke to him for quite a while, asking about the way his village prospered and promising to pass no harsh laws.

After speaking to her, Franz felt that Forestia must have the best queen in the whole world.

But then, of course, the queen had to ride on and Franz had to go back to his work.

Chatting to important people is very thrilling, but it doesn't earn the money to buy the food to feed hungry mouths. And there are always plenty of hungry mouths about, as any mummy or daddy will tell you.

Anyway, the next day, Franz went to work in much the same place—in the

clearing next to the main pathway through the forest.

All morning Franz worked, then at midday he stopped for a snack of bread and cheese—and, if truth be told, for a little doze under the bushes, where no one could see him and tell him he ought to be getting on with his work and what about feeding those hungry mouths?

Well, while Franz was dozing, two more grand travellers happened along and, seeing the nice clearing, they decided to stop for *their* midday snack.

But then instead of dozing, like Franz, these two travellers started chatting. If only they had dozed, they would still be going happily about their business —wicked business though it was.

You see, these two men were uncles to the queen and they were plotting to rob her of her jewels and if that went well, to capture the queen herself, lock her up for ever and rule Forestia in her place.

But luckily for the queen all this chattering woke Franz up and he heard what the uncles were plotting.

"How wicked!" thought Franz. "I must warn the queen at once." But being very clever, as well as a light sleeper, Franz kept quiet and still until the uncles had ridden off. So the uncles did not know they had been overheard.

Now, of course, if you are a simple chap who has lived in the forest all your life, you are not very familiar with the ways of the world and you are certainly not very familiar with the way to reach a royal palace and get in to see the queen.

Franz just dashed straight off towards the big city, as he was, in his grubby working clothes.

And then by the time he had lost his way, slept in a barn over night and had a couple of fights with robbers, he certainly looked pretty scruffy when he arrived outside the palace and said he wanted to see the queen.

"Ha! Ha! Yes, and I want to have tea with the Major General," laughed the soldier on duty, "but I'm not going to. And you are not going to see the queen. Be off with you, you country bumpkin."

But though Franz was certainly from the country, he was no bumpkin, as we have seen before.

Franz went to ask advice from the Wise Woman of the Woods.

"Well, of course, a little soap and water never hurts anyone," advised the Wise Woman—and when Franz was looking neat again, the Wise Woman pointed up at the birds flying swiftly through the sky.

"Birds can fly anywhere," smiled the Wise Woman. "Certainly they can fly over the heads of cheeky soldiers and over the tops of palace walls and in through open windows and on to the shoulders of beautiful ladies."

She was quite a chatterbox, as well as being wise, you see. Luckily she was also skilled in magic and she turned Franz into a beautiful golden bird.

"Thank you," called Franz, who was still able to talk like a human being and he flew away from the cottage of the Wise Woman of the Woods, over the head of the cheeky soldier, over the palace walls and in through the open window of the room where the queen was sitting.

The queen was delighted to see such a beautiful golden bird, but horrified at the story the bird sang in her ear.

She sent for her uncles at once and they were so surprised they admitted all the wicked deeds they had been planning.

"You are banished from my kingdom for ever," ordered the queen. And the wicked uncles were so glad to be let off so lightly, they never returned again.

And then the beautiful golden bird turned back into being Franz and the queen made him rich for life, which pleased him and the rest of his family, who never had to worry about being hungry again. They all always had plenty of food. Hooray!

Twelve Dancing Princesses

Once upon a time there was a king who had twelve daughters and each one was more beautiful than the other.

These twelve lovely princesses all slept together in a large room in the royal palace.

Every night when the princesses went to bed, the king turned the key and locked their bedroom door but every morning when the king unlocked the door, he had a surprise.

The princesses were asleep in their beds but their shoes, which had been new the night before, were quite worn through.

How had the princesses worn out their shoes when they had been locked in their room all night?

The king couldn't understand it—and the princesses wouldn't say.

They were quite sure that if the king knew what they were doing, he would stop them from doing it, so the princesses all pretended that they were as puzzled about the shoes as anyone.

Now, all this was very irritating to the king, because kings like to know everything.

A proclamation would be sent out, the king decided, saying that any man who could discover how the princesses' shoes were worn out during the night could choose one of his daughters to be his wife and, one day, would become king and rule the kingdom in his place. Whoever tried to find out and failed after three nights, however, would have to spend the rest of his life in prison.

One might imagine that no one would wish to take such a terrible chance, but soon a prince came knocking at the palace door and said that he was willing to try to find out the secret.

The king was well pleased because the prince seemed a handsome, intelligent young fellow.

The prince was given a good supper by the king and then sent to sleep outside the princesses' door, which was left open.

Now, of course, the prince was only supposed to pretend to sleep and really he was meant to stay awake but the good supper he had eaten made him so drowsy that he slept all night.

Alas! In the morning the princesses' shoes were worn into holes—as usual—and the prince didn't know why.

But there were still two more nights.

However, on both those nights the princesses slipped sleeping powder into the prince's wine and he slept heavily till daylight.

The morning after the third night, the prince was put into prison. Poor fellow!

Well, hardly surprisingly, for a long time after that no one else offered to try to solve the riddle of the shoes. But one day a travelling soldier fell to chatting with an old lady.

"I will tell you how to solve the mystery of the princesses' worn-out shoes," smiled the old lady. "Go to the palace but do not drink the wine given to you in the evening and when you wish to follow the princesses, put on this cloak, which will make you invisible."

So the soldier went to the palace and asked the king if he might try to discover the secret of the worn-out shoes. Although the king was not so keen on having a penniless soldier marry one of his daughters, he agreed to let the soldier try. The king was tired of buying so many new shoes, you see.

The king invited the soldier into the palace, gave him a splendid meal and took

him to where he would sleep outside the door of the princesses' bedchamber, just as the poor prince had done.

Remembering the advice of the old lady, the soldier did not drink the wine which, of course, contained some sleeping powder. The soldier settled down on his bed and just pretended to go to sleep.

When the princesses heard the soldier gently snoring, they leapt out of their beds.

"We have tricked this soldier just as we tricked that stupid prince," they laughed rather heartlessly and then they put on their prettiest dresses and, of course, they put on their shoes.

Then the eldest princess knocked upon one of the beds and it sank into the floor to reveal a staircase. Laughing happily, the twelve princesses scampered downwards.

At once, the soldier wrapped the magic cloak about him so that he was invisible and he followed the princesses.

Halfway down the staircase, the soldier trod on the skirt of the youngest princess. She was frightened and called: "Someone is tugging at my dress."

But the other princesses told her she was being silly. "Your dress only caught on a nail," they laughed.

Down, down they all went, until they stood in a marvellous avenue of trees. All the trees were made of silver and glittered and shone in the eerie underground light.

The soldier thought, "I must take a token with me to prove to the king that I'm telling the truth," and he broke a silver twig from a tree.

The twig gave a sharp crack and the youngest princess called: "All is not well. Did you hear that crack?" But the others just laughed at her again.

Next they came to an avenue where all the leaves were of gold and then to a third avenue where the leaves were of diamonds. From these avenues, too, the soldier broke a twig and each time the youngest princess started with fright.

Faster and faster went the princesses till they came to a lake. By the lakeside were twelve boats and in each boat sat a handsome prince. Each princess climbed into a boat and the soldier slipped into the boat with the youngest princess.

At once the princes rowed across the lake towards a brilliantly lighted palace.

The princes were brothers and under a spell cast on them by a wicked magician they had to live underground until the princesses' secret was discovered.

All night long in the dazzling palace the princesses danced with the handsome princes. Then just before dawn, the princesses dressed as ballerinas for a special dance. The youngest princess looked so beautiful that the soldier made up his mind that she would be his wife.

Then on danced the princes and princesses until the princesses' shoes were worn through. Quickly, they left and the princes rowed them back across the lake.

This time the soldier slipped into the boat carrying the eldest princess because she would be first back to the palace.

When they reached the shore, the princes said farewell to the princesses and promised to meet the following night.

Then, while the princesses were trudging wearily up the stairs, the soldier ran ahead, took off his magic cloak, climbed into bed and pretended to be asleep.

The princesses looked at the sleeping soldier and were quite sure he had not learned their secret.

The following two nights, the same thing happened. The soldier wore his magic cloak and followed the princesses and watched everything that took place. On the last night, he even stole a wine cup to show to the king.

The next morning the soldier told the king everything.

"Ah! We are betrayed," gasped the princesses and the beautiful underground palace across the lake crumbled to pieces and the handsome princes were released from the spell that kept them prisoner and happily they returned to their homes.

The soldier and the youngest princess were married and after many years, as the old king had promised, the soldier became king and ruled the land.

The Nail

"Tra-la-la! Happy days! Let's all enjoy ourselves!"

So sang a jolly merchant, who lived long ago and who had lots of money.

Every day the merchant would ride out, tossing money to any poor people he saw, as his carriage bowled along.

"I don't want to see any long faces round me," chuckled the merchant. "Never worry about what might happen tomorrow."

As you may have guessed, it was the merchant's *father* who had worked hard making all the money, not the merchant himself. He had just had the money given to him.

Never mind! The merchant was a happy chap and who shall begrudge him that?

But being always cheery and looking on the *bright* side can have its *bad* side.

One day, just as they were setting out for a drive, the coachman said to the merchant: "There is a loose nail in one of the horses' shoes."

"Oh, never mind about that," laughed the merchant. "The sun is shining, the birds are singing—why bother about little things like nails?"

So off they drove into the country. But when they had gone a few miles the horse with the loose nail lost a shoe.

"One of the horses has cast a shoe, sir," said the coachman to the merchant.

"Don't be gloomy. Look on the bright side," laughed the merchant. "Say the horses still have seven *good* shoes."

But a little further on the horse which had cast its shoe stumbled and then it fell and broke its leg and it pulled the other horse down with it. The merchant was forced to leave the coach and he and the coachman had to walk home—and all for want of a nail and a little forethought.

29

The Three Soldiers

Now in the olden days things were very different from the way they are now.

When wars were over, the soldiers weren't brought home and given a nice suit of clothes and an allowance of money until they could find good jobs.

Dear me no. In those bad old days, the general or prince or whoever was in charge of the army would just call the soldiers together and say: "Well, thanks very much, chaps, and goodbye."

Then the soldiers had to find their own ways home as best they could, as these

the dwarf—and then he was gone.

Later that night, the second soldier sat on guard by the fire and the dwarf came and spoke to him and gave him a purse which would always contain gold.

What a handsome present!

Then a little later on still, when the third soldier was on duty, the dwarf gave him a horn.

"Whenever you play a tune upon this horn, great crowds will gather round you and dance merrily to the music," said the dwarf.

Perhaps this wasn't such a fine present as the first two, but at least the third soldier need never be lonely!

Anyway, in the morning, the three soldiers showed each other their presents and they were very pleased. Between the cloak and the purse and the horn, they should always be able to have everything they wanted in life.

"Perhaps our hard days are over and the good times have arrived," they smiled.

three brave soldiers are doing.

Many a long, footsore mile the three soldiers trudged, trying to find their way back to their homeland. And of course, as they had no money, at night they had to sleep out on the cold hard ground. It was just no fun at all and it was only the friendship the soldiers had for each other that kept them going.

Well, one weary night the soldiers were sleeping in a forest. At least two of them were sleeping—and the other was keeping guard. For however little you have, there is always someone ready to steal that little from you.

However, it wasn't a thief who came near the soldiers that night, it was a strange dwarf.

The soldier who was on guard smiled at the dwarf. "We are just three poor soldiers," he said, "but you are welcome to share the warmth of our fire, if you wish."

"How very kind of you," smiled the dwarf, settling gratefully by the fire. He had only been there a few minutes, when he took out a cloak and gave it to the soldier. "When you wear this cloak anything you wish for will be granted," said

Little did they know!

There were still many perils lying in the path of the three brave soldiers, but for the moment they could see no problems.

The first soldier stood up and put the dwarf's cloak round his shoulders. He looked at the road stretching mile after mile ahead of them through the forest.

"The first thing we need," he smiled, "is a fine coach in which to ride because I am certainly tired of walking."

In a moment a grand coach appeared at the roadside with two strong horses and a man to drive them.

The soldiers were thrilled!

"What rich folk we are now," they laughed, bowing to each other. And they hustled into the coach and drove to the nearest big town.

There they took gold from the second soldier's purse and ate a huge meal at the best inn in town and then they bought themselves lots of suits of elegant clothes.

How very happy they were!

"Now," they smiled, "our next task is to find a pleasant place in which to live."

So the soldiers journeyed on, staying a few days here and a few weeks there, until

they came to a very pleasant kingdom where the king invited them to dinner.

You see, by now the three soldiers appeared to be noblemen, their way of life was so expensive—thanks to the gifts of the dwarf.

Now the king who had invited the soldiers to dinner had a daughter called Griselda.

What a funny, old-fashioned name that does sound to us, doesn't it? I wonder if her friends called her Grizzley for short?

I don't suppose so. Griselda was a princess and no one would have dared to call her by a nickname.

Anyway, Princess Griselda was not only pretty, she was also clever in a rather sneaky, cunning sort of way.

Princess Griselda felt very curious to know how the three soldiers came to be so rich.

"They don't speak of big estates from which they could get rent," she thought, "and they don't carry big treasure chests with them—and yet they always have

plenty of money. Where does it come from?"

Princess Griselda made up her mind that she would find out.

So Griselda waited until the three soldiers had eaten a wonderful meal and were feeling happy and chatty.

Griselda moved close to the second soldier, who was listening to her father.

"And do you know why the chicken crossed the road?" the king was asking.

"No," chuckled the soldier, who was the second soldier, who had been given the purse, "why did the chicken cross the road?"

"To get to the other side, of course," laughed the king. And the soldier laughed too.

"Well, if he is in the mood to laugh at old jokes like that, then he is in the mood to tell secrets," thought Griselda.

She took the second soldier to sit in a quiet corner of the garden.

"Do you know, I think you are wonderfully clever," she told the second soldier.

"Really?" smiled the soldier, feeling very flattered. "Why is that?"

"Well," went on Griselda, "whenever my father, the king, and I travel to distant lands, we have to carry our money in heavy chests, which have to be carried in strong waggons, pulled by big horses. And the horses have to have grooms and the waggons have to have drivers and they all need soldiers to guard them and they all need cooks to supply their food. Oh, the trouble is never ending. But you and your two friends don't seem to have any of these problems. You just travel in a coach with one driver—and yet you always have plenty of money. That is why I say you are clever."

The soldier felt a little embarrassed.

"Oh, it's not all that clever, really," he muttered.

Then as the princess seemed so nice and everyone at the palace was so friendly, the soldier thought it would not hurt to tell the secret of his wealth.

What a mistake!

"Really we are three poor soldiers," prattled the soldier, "but one night we met a nice dwarf and he gave me this purse, which is always full of gold and he gave my friends a cloak, which will grant any wish and a horn which will always make lots of people gather round to listen to its music."

"How interesting. Do go on," smiled Princess Griselda, her eyes gleaming greedily at the sight of the gold in the purse.

So the soldier put the purse back in his pocket and babbled on foolishly to Princess Griselda about the grand clothes they had bought and the fine meals they had eaten and what fun it was to have as much money as you wanted.

Princess Griselda did not need any convincing of that.

She was already making sure that she would always have plenty of money—by stealing the dwarf's purse from the soldier's pocket. I'm afraid being a princess does not stop a young lady from being naughty.

She hid the purse amongst her long skirts and led the silly soldier back to the banqueting room.

"Do try this new ice-cream," she smiled. "The recipe has just arrived from Italy."

Well, the foolish young soldier did not notice that the purse was gone and at the end of the evening he and his two friends went back to their lodgings.

But of course the time came when they needed some money to pay their bills. Then the soldier searched for the purse in vain. He remembered that the last time he had seen it was when he had shown it to Princess Griselda.

"Can the Princess Griselda have stolen the purse?" he gasped. "Why, she is rich already."

"No matter how much money a person has, they can still long for more," said the first soldier, who was wiser than the second soldier.

He picked up his magic cloak.

"I will magic myself into the palace to see if the princess really has the purse and if she has, then I will seize it back again," he said.

Proving that, wise though he was, he didn't know much about princesses nor palaces.

Snatching magic purses from princesses is easier said than done.

However—POP!

As soon as the soldier put the cloak round his shoulders and wished to be standing near the princess—there he was.

And there was Princess Griselda tipping gold coins out of the magic purse and laughing.

"Give that back at once, you naughty young lady," snapped the soldier indignantly.

But, of course, it is no use speaking sharply to princesses—especially not in palaces filled with armed men.

"HELP! GUARDS!" shrieked the princess, slamming the purse away in a drawer.

And before the soldier could gather his wits together, great, big, fierce palace guards and the head butler and the king all came rushing in waving sticks and guns and swords.

How very frightening!

The soldier jumped straight out of the nearest window—very quickly!

Bump! Scramble! Bonk!

The poor soldier landed in a tree and slithered down through the branches till he hit the ground.

And needless to say the magic cloak was left tangled in the branches just outside Princess Griselda's window.

The soldier looked up just in time to see the princess lean out and take the cloak.

"I think I'll have this," she smiled. "Every princess should have a magic cloak hanging in her wardrobe."

Of course the soldier was FURIOUS, but then out from the palace pelted the huge soldiers and the head butler and the king, still looking fierce and waving their guns and swords and sticks.

The second soldier made the wise decision to run for his life and he just managed to escape back to his two friends.

But by now the three soldiers were in a sorry plight.

The gold-filled purse was gone. The magic cloak was gone. The only thing left of the dwarf's gifts was the magic horn.

"Well, perhaps the horn will get us out of our troubles," smiled the third soldier. "I will play a military tune on the horn and perhaps lots of soldiers will gather round."

Well, it seemed that good fortune was still smiling on the three soldiers after all.

As the third soldier played on the horn, a huge army of soldiers gathered round and said they would do anything they could to help the three soldiers.

The soldiers were very pleased. They lined their new army up outside the palace where Princess Griselda lived.

"Let's send in a message to say that if that no-good Griselda doesn't give back the things she has stolen, we will come in and chop off her head," suggested the first soldier, who was very angry.

But by now the second soldier had learnt that one must be polite to princesses, even naughty ones, because princesses have so many important friends.

"Let us say that if that no-good *beautiful Princess* Griselda doesn't give back the things she has stolen, we will come in and chop off her head, *when convenient*," he suggested.

"Charmingly put," agreed the others. And so the message was sent.

But it didn't work.

Princess Griselda was too clever for them.

First Griselda sent a message to say she would think their interesting suggestion over—which sounded quite promising, so the soldiers sat down to wait. But while they were dozing, the princess sneaked out and stole the magic horn—and at once—PUFF! All the great army disappeared and the three soldiers were left alone and forlorn.

"Be off with you," shouted the princess and the soldiers had no choice but to go. They were back as they were before they had met the dwarf.

Anyway, after they had trudged a few miles, the soldier who had once owned the purse decided he would branch off on his own.

So he said farewell to his companions and turned off to walk through an orchard. Now walking is hungry work and when the soldier saw a tree with particularly crunchy-looking apples on it, he couldn't help stopping and thinking how nice it would be to eat an apple for his lunch.

"Surely no one would begrudge a poor soldier an apple or two," he thought.

Now, the soldier really should not have taken the apples, because they did not belong to him, but as Princess Griselda had not been fussy about taking things that did not belong to her, the soldier did

not see why he should be fussy either.

The soldier had no sooner taken a bite of the apple than his nose started to grow and grow and GROW!

How upsetting—and frightening—and INCONVENIENT!

The soldier was HORRIFIED!

"Everyone will laugh at me," he gasped, "and I shall never get a job again. Who will employ a soldier with a long nose?"

The soldier sat at the foot of the tree feeling more and more upset.

A bird even came and perched on the nose, thinking it was a long branch.

The bird looked along the branch, as she thought, towards the soldier.

"What a very strange-looking tree," she twittered. "I suppose it is some new modern type."

The bird sighed heavily.

"I liked the old-fashioned trees best," she twirped. "Why does everything have to keep changing? I don't know what the world is coming to."

"For heaven's sake," gasped the poor soldier, "do stop moaning. I'm the one with problems, not you."

"TALKING TREES!" shrieked the bird. "I can't bear it."

And she flew away and never went near that orchard again.

But, as the old saying goes: The darkest hour is just before the dawn, which means that just when things seem at their worst, they are really about to get better again.

The poor soldier was sitting there looking dismally at his nose, which was still growing longer and longer, when who

should come by but his two old friends.

"We were lonely without you, so we came to look for you," they smiled.

But their expressions changed when they saw their friend's long nose.

"Whatever has happened?" they gasped.

"Oh, how I wish I knew," sighed the second soldier. "All I did was take a bite from this apple and at once my nose started to grow and GROW!"

How sorry the soldier's two friends felt, but they didn't know what to do to help.

The three old friends were all sitting under the apple tree, feeling really glum, when there was a flash of burning light and standing in front of them was a little dwarf. The same dwarf who had helped them before.

"Hallo there," he smiled.

Then he looked at their doleful appearance and at the second soldier's long nose.

"I have no wish to interfere where I am not wanted," he said, "but you do look as if you need some help."

So then the unhappy soldiers told the dwarf all about what had happened to the three gifts he had given them and of course finished up by saying that the very worst thing that had happened to them was the long nose growing on the second soldier.

"Aha, but that is where you are wrong," smiled the dwarf. "This long nose will show you the way to win back all your other treasures.

"Eating this apple made your nose grow long," explained the dwarf, "but eating one of these pears will make your nose shrink to the right size again."

And he picked a pear growing on another tree in the orchard.

"Oh, please, give me the pear at once," begged the soldier and taking the pear he ate it and his nose shrank and the soldier felt happier than he had ever felt in his life before.

"Thank you, Mr. Dwarf," he sighed.

But then the other two soldiers said, "How can all this help us to get back the purse and cloak and horn stolen from us by that naughty Princess Griselda?"

So the dwarf explained a very clever plan to the three soldiers and smiling happily the soldiers picked some fruit from the trees and hurried back towards the palace where Princess Griselda lived.

Just before they reached the palace, the dwarf gave the second soldier a basket and some clothes to make him look like a gardener's boy. Then at last all was ready.

The second soldier put the magic apples into the basket and went to stand outside the palace.

The apples looked so delicious that everyone wanted to buy them.

"No," said the second soldier, "these marvellous apples are fit for a princess only. I have brought the apples as a present for Princess Griselda."

A serving maid stepped forward.

"I am maid to the Princess Griselda," she said. "If you give the apples to me, I will see that they reach the princess."

So the second soldier gave the apples to

the serving maid, warning her that no one but the princess must eat them.

Now, luckily for her, the maid was honest. She didn't try to eat the apples herself, but took them straight to her royal mistress.

Princess Griselda was thrilled with the fresh, crunchy-looking apples.

"Why our stupid gardeners can't grow apples as nice as this, I don't know," she said in her horrid way and took a big bite from one of the apples.

AAAAAGH! Immediately the princess's nose grew and grew.

She was horrified.

The maid was terrified.

The king was sent for.

"Do something! Send for someone! HELP!" shrieked the poor king.

So a proclamation was read outside the palace, stating that anyone who knew how to shrink extra long noses should come to see the king at once.

No one mentioned that the *princess* had a long nose. That sort of scandal is best kept quiet.

Well, when the three soldiers heard the royal proclamation, they were thrilled. Their plan was working perfectly.

The third soldier, the one who had once

owned the horn, dressed up as a doctor and, carrying one of the pears, went into the palace and said he knew all about shrinking noses.

He was taken to see the princess at once.

"Oh yes," he smiled, "there is no need to worry, I can soon cure that long nose—charming though it looks, of course."

He was still remembering that one must always be polite to princesses.

Then he scratched his head.

"Dear me!" he gasped. "I have such a dreadful memory. Do you know, instead of being able to remember the cure for long noses, all I can think of are some friends of mine who have had a purse and a cloak and a horn stolen—er borrowed—from them. Until those things are given back, I don't think I shall be able to cure this long—er charming—nose."

At once the princess told the maid where to find the purse and cloak and horn and to give them to the doctor.

When the three precious gifts were safely in his possession, the doctor—or rather the third soldier—gave the pear to the princess and told her to eat it.

And as soon as the princess ate the pear, her nose shrank back to its normal size.

How wonderful!

The princess was so happy to be pretty again, as a princess should be.

The maid was delighted, because now she could not be blamed for having brought the apples to the princess.

The king was thrilled to see his beloved daughter happy again.

And none of the three gave a glance or a thought to the doctor, as he raised his hat and left the palace.

Back to his two friends scampered the doctor, who was, of course, the third soldier.

He gave the first soldier the magic cloak and to the second soldier he gave the magic purse and he himself kept the magic horn.

Then they hurried away to find a kingdom without such a naughty princess and they settled down and lived quite happily ever after.

The Bamboo Princess

Far away in Japan there once lived an elderly man and his wife. Their little wooden house stood by a swift-flowing river and behind it were hills, covered with bamboo and fir trees. The couple made a poor living by cutting down the bamboo and weaving it into vases and baskets. These they took to the nearest town and sold.

However, as they grew older, the couple grew more and more lonely. "If only we had a child to bring us joy and happiness," the wife would sigh.

One day, in early springtime, the old man went out as usual to the bamboo thicket to chop down the bamboo canes. He had not been working long when he noticed that one of the canes was swaying around in a very odd manner. There was no wind and all the other canes were still. Only this one was moving.

"This must be a very special cane," thought the old man and with one swipe from his sharp knife he cut it to the ground.

He picked up the fallen cane, thinking what a fine basket it would make, when he felt the cane moving in his hands. How very strange. Such a thing had never happened before.

Very carefully, the old man slit the cane open and there, lying inside the bamboo, was a tiny girl.

She had soft, white skin and jet black hair and she was dressed in a tiny silk kimono, with a silk sash.

Such fine clothes had never been seen by the old man before in his life.

"We have been sent the baby of our dreams," smiled the bamboo cutter and he took the little girl home to his wife.

The wife was as pleased as the old man and loved the little foundling child.

Now, as might be supposed, a child found in a bamboo shoot did not grow as other children do.

Before the moon was full the new baby had grown to be two feet tall and the rich kimono was far too small for her.

"It is no use dressing this beautiful girl in poor clothes," said the bamboo cutter's wife. "We must buy her clothes as rich as the ones in which you found her."

So the poor old couple spent all their savings on rich silk to clothe their strange child—and still the little girl grew and grew.

She was beautiful, but she was certainly a problem!

Finally, when there was just no money left, the bamboo cutter went to the bamboo grove as usual, his mind filled with worries about where his next penny would come from. Suddenly a stream of gold coins poured from a bamboo he had just felled.

How very nice!

The old man was thrilled.

"Whoever sent the little girl has sent the money with which to keep her," he smiled.

So after that the old man and his wife could be happy with no worries. No matter how their foundling child grew, they had the money to clothe and feed her.

By the time she was three years old the girl was like a seventeen-year-old young lady and her fame was spreading far and wide.

In fact the Bamboo Princess, as she came to be called, was so famous and beautiful that many young men wished to marry her.

The old couple talked things over and decided that as they would not live for ever, it really would be right for the

Bamboo Princess to marry and have her own home.

So of all the young men who came courting the Bamboo Princess, the old couple chose the three most handsome and most wealthy and asked the princess to choose one to be her husband.

The Bamboo Princess sighed. "I don't really want to get married at all," she said, "But I will set each young man a task and if one fulfils his task, I will marry him."

To the first young man the Bamboo Princess said: "Fetch me the bowl which has been used by the Lord Buddha both as a drinking and a begging bowl."

To the second young man she said: "Bring me the fireproof skin of the tree rats which live over the Western Sea."

And to the third young man she said: "Bring me the sea-shell which the swallows are said to keep hidden in their nests."

Well, the three young men set off bravely promising that they would do anything to win the hand of the beautiful Bamboo Princess, but the more they thought about the tasks she had set, the more they didn't want to do them.

"Why should I go grubbing across half China looking for one particular bowl?" thought the first young man. "Surely any bowl will do. After all, that girl has never been out of her own village. How does she know what the Lord Buddha's bowl looks like?"

So the first young man went to a potter and had a fine bowl made and took that to the Bamboo Princess.

But the Bamboo Princess looked at the bowl and shook her head.

"This is not the bowl of the Lord Buddha," she said. "Be off with you, young man."

Now while this had been going on, the second young man had been standing looking at the Western Sea and the more he looked at it, the colder and wetter and rougher it appeared.

"Well, I'm certainly not sailing all the way across that just to fetch a few rat furs," thought the young man to himself.

"One rat is just like another, if you ask me."

So the second young man went to a furrier and asked him to make up a fireproof fur of rat skins.

But, of course, when the Bamboo Princess saw the fur, she knew it had not come from over the Western Sea.

"You haven't even had time to sail across the Western Sea, let alone come back again," she said to the young man.

So he went away, thinking that a wife as clever as that might not have suited him anyway.

And as for the third young man, he soon grew tired of scrambling up on high, looking into swallows' nests and he just bought a shell from a fisherman and gave that to the Bamboo Princess.

"*That* is not the shell I had in mind," said the Bamboo Princess, so the third young man was sent on his way.

But then another and much more important young man came to court the Bamboo Princess. He was the heir to the Imperial Japanese throne.

"Surely," thought the old couple, "the Bamboo Princess will want to marry this young man."

But she didn't. However, as he was so important, the Bamboo Princess felt she owed the heir to the throne an explanation for her refusal and she gave him a long scroll of paper on which were written beautifully formed characters. The prince read it, sighed deeply and left the house.

Then the Bamboo Princess turned to the old couple. "Dear parents," she said, "I am really the daughter of the Moon. For being rude and unkind my father banished me to Earth. He made me very small and hid me in a bamboo shoot. You found me and cared for me and now that you have shown me what goodness is, I can return to live with my father amongst the stars."

And at the full moon—she left.

All that remained of her on Earth was the scroll given to the heir to the Japanese throne and he took it to the top of Mount Fuji and burnt it and it smoulders there to this day.

If it had not been for Judar, the youngest son, the family would certainly have starved.

Judar was a very clever fisherman and every day he would go to the river and catch fish to feed his own family and to sell.

Then with the money he gained from selling the fish, Judar would buy the other things that the family needed to live.

Not that his brothers were grateful. "Fish, fish, fish!" they would moan. "We'll grow scales if we have to eat many more of the stupid things."

But then, as so often happens, the day came when there were no more fish in the river.

Either they had all been caught or they had decided to live somewhere else. No one

The Magic Treasure

Many, many years ago, in a far, far distant country, there lived a merchant called Omar. This merchant had three sons. The eldest was called Salem, the second Seleem and the youngest Judar.

Now, as must always happen, the day came when Omar died and the three sons were left to look after their mother.

Well, one would have thought that three strapping young men could easily look after a home and one old lady—and indeed they could—if the three strapping young men had worked hard.

But they didn't.

Salem, the eldest, and Seleem, the middle son, didn't believe in work. They just sat around all day grumbling about having to eat plain food and not being able to have new clothes, because their father had died and there was no more money coming in.

ever knew—but there were no more to catch. Poor Judar!

And indeed poor Salem and poor Seleem and poor mother! Because now there was no income of any sort.

But instead of thinking that perhaps now it was *their* turn to work, the brothers grumbled at Judar.

"Well, don't just stand there," they shouted. "The fish won't come here looking for *you,* you know. Try to find fish in some other river."

So off Judar went.

Several days' journey from his home, Judar came upon a dark and mysterious lake and standing by the lake, almost as if he were waiting for Judar, was a rich looking stranger.

"Oh, hallo, Judar," he smiled, "my name is Abdul Samad and I need your help. I want you to bind my hands and feet and throw me into the lake. When I come to the surface again, I want you to pull me out with your net. Do this and I will make you rich."

It all seemed very strange, not least the fact that the stranger knew Judar's name, but Judar decided to do as he was asked—after all, he might catch some fish at the same time.

There was a loud SPLASH!

Into the lake went the rich stranger and—POP!—up he came again.

This time he was clutching two large fish.

"These are magic fish who will lead me to the Treasure House of Al-Shamardal," gurgled the rich stranger, "and in the Treasure House are a Magic Sword, a Magic Ring, a Magic Bottle and a Glass Ball. With these four things I can rule the world, but I shall need your help again, Judar."

And with that the stranger tossed Judar a bag of gold and rode off.

Judar was, of course, very pleased and hurried home to show the gold to his mother and brothers.

"Now we have enough money to live well for months," they all smiled happily.

But money never lasts as long as one thinks it will and soon the bag of gold was empty.

"I think I had better go in search of Abdul Samad, the rich stranger," said Judar.

"Yes, indeed," replied Salem and Seleem. "Fancy idling your time round

The plan worked well. After another long journey and many adventures, Judar, dressed in his fine new clothes, and Abdul reached the Treasure House of Al-Shamardal.

Judar strode boldly forward and demanded to be let in—and the guards let him pass. It was the same inside the Treasure House. Every door was opened until Judar reached the door of the room where Al-Shamardal was asleep.

Round Al-Shamardal's neck hung the Magic Bottle, above his head shone the Magic Glass Ball and on his finger glittered the Magic Ring and at his feet lay the Magic Sword.

Hardly daring to breathe and with his heart pounding, Judar crept forward and took all the treasure so desired by Abdul.

Then he walked bravely from the palace and no one questioned his going.

Outside the Magic Treasure House, Abdul greeted Judar with joy and together

here when you could be finding treasure. Be off with you, you lazy chap."

So off to the lake journeyed Judar and there was Abdul Samad waiting, just as before.

"Ah, hallo, Judar," smiled Abdul, "how nice to see you. Are you ready to help me enter the Treasure House of Al-Shamardal?"

"Yes, sir, if it will gain me riches to take home to my mother," replied Judar.

"Good lad," smiled Abdul. "Follow me." And Abdul led Judar on a long, long journey, which ended at a grand palace.

"This is my home," smiled Abdul. He took Judar into the palace, where he met Abdul's beautiful daughter and ate a grand feast and then was given suits of most magnificent clothes.

"You need these clothes to gain entrance to the Treasure House of Al-Shamardal," explained Abdul. "You see, Judar, by good fortune you look just like the son of Al-Shamardal, so with luck the guards will let you into the Treasure House with no trouble but only if you are dressed as Al-Shamardal's son is usually dressed, of course."

time. All the family's money had been spent and his mother was cold and hungry —because, of course, the brothers had not given a thought to working.

"You took your time," snapped the brothers to Judar. "Why, if you had been gone another day, we should have had to send mother out to scrub floors. We don't know how you could be so inconsiderate."

Well, even Judar felt a little annoyed at that, but he had to love his brothers for his mother's sake.

So Judar bought his brothers a nice house *next door* to the lovely house he bought for his mother and himself, so his mother could visit the brothers, but Judar didn't have to listen to their grumblings.

Then Judar and his mother lived happily ever after and every time they felt hungry, Judar just opened the magic leather pouch and took out the tastiest, most delicious food that his mother had ever seen.

"You are a good son, Judar," smiled his mother.

they hurried back to Abdul's palace.

The Magic Treasure was carefully hidden away and then Abdul sat on a magnificent chair and smiled.

"Now I shall be the most powerful man on earth," he sighed happily, "and the first thing I must do is reward you for helping me, Judar. Tell me what you would like as a present."

Now, on his journeyings with Abdul, Judar had noticed that Abdul had a leather pouch from which he could always take food. The pouch was never empty and the food was always fresh. It was a magic pouch, of course.

"Please give me the pouch which is never empty of food," asked Judar, "then my mother and brothers will never be short of something to eat."

"Gladly," agreed Abdul, "and as well as that I will give you gold and jewels to make you a rich man."

How pleased Judar was.

So Judar took the rich gifts and hurried home to his mother. He arrived just in

ALADDIN

Long, long ago and many miles away in a wild country of deserts and mountains and a few green river valleys lived a boy called Aladdin.

Once Aladdin's life had been quite comfortable and happy, but that had been before his father, Mustapha the tailor, had died.

Now Aladdin's mother was a poor widow and life was rather grim.

Somehow there was never quite enough money to buy all the food they needed and never quite enough wood to burn to keep Aladdin and his mother warm in the cold weather.

"Ah, well, never mind," Aladdin's mother would smile, "we still have each other—and something nice is sure to turn up sometime."

And one day something nice did turn up—or so it seemed at the time.

The whole adventure started when Aladdin went out looking for work. He had only trotted a few paces when a grand stranger came up to him and said:

"Who are you, my lad?"

"I am Aladdin, the son of Mustapha the tailor," replied Aladdin.

"I thought so," smiled the stranger. "Why, you are the image of your father. Now just hurry home, my boy, and tell your mother that I will be round in a few minutes to visit her."

Aladdin's mother was quite puzzled. She didn't know any grand folk at all, but she prepared for a visitor as best she could in her poor way.

But when the stranger arrived he brought a servant with him carrying the most magnificent food.

"I am Mustapha's long lost brother and all your troubles are over," he smiled.

51

How amazing!

And it was especially amazing as Aladdin's mother had never heard that her husband Mustapha had a brother at all!

But the stranger was so friendly and kind and generous that it really seemed foolish to seek to find fault with him.

Aladdin's uncle, as it seemed the stranger was, bought new clothes for Aladdin and his mother, stocked the house with food and fuel for the cold weather and even bought Aladdin a fine horse.

How very pleasant life had become. If only everything the stranger said had been true!

But alas!

The stranger was not speaking the truth at all. He was not Aladdin's uncle. He was a wicked magician and he was only being so friendly because he needed Aladdin's help.

Well, several happy days of plenty passed by and then Aladdin's so-called uncle invited Aladdin to go for a ride in the mountains on the fine new horse.

"Listen carefully, Aladdin," said the magician, as they rode along. "If you do just as I say, you will become very rich, richer even than I am—if that is possible!"

"I will do as you say, uncle," smiled

Aladdin, because he was quite sure that his uncle was a good and kind man.

Poor Aladdin!

There he was being so trustful and the man he was with wasn't even his uncle, let alone good and kind.

However, they rode up into the mountains till they came to the spot that the magician sought.

"We will dismount from our horses here," smiled the magician, "and I will build a fire."

This did not bother Aladdin. He merely thought his uncle was going to cook some food—but then—WHAT A SURPRISE!

The magician threw some powder on to the fire and the ground began to crack and tremble.

Dense smoke swirled all around and when it cleared, Aladdin saw a flat stone set into the ground with an iron ring embedded in it.

Aladdin was looking at a TRAPDOOR!

The magician acted as if nothing unusual had happened at all.

"Aladdin, my boy," he smiled, "just lift up that trapdoor and pop down the steps that you will see, there's a good chap."

"Go down the steps," went on the magician, "and you will find yourself in a

beautiful garden. There you will find a rusty old lamp. Now listen carefully—you are to bring that lamp straight back to me. Understand?"

"Yes, uncle," replied Aladdin. He was rather surprised to see a greedy expression on his uncle's face.

"Good lad," smiled the magician greasily. "I appreciate your help very much indeed." He slipped a cheap-looking brass ring from his finger and handed it to Aladdin. "Here, Aladdin, take this for all your trouble."

He did not tell Aladdin that the brass ring was in fact a magic ring, neither did he tell him that the lamp was a magic lamp. He thought that Aladdin was far too stupid to understand magical matters.

The magician, during one of his many strange adventures, had once been trapped in an underground cave and had only narrowly escaped with his life. Ever since then he had always avoided underground caves and that was why he wanted Aladdin to go down and fetch him the lamp.

But Aladdin remembered that greedy expression on his uncle's face and when he found the lamp, an uneasy feeling prompted him to say, "I think I'll keep this old lamp for myself, uncle."

In sudden rage the magician slammed down the trapdoor. Aladdin was trapped! For hours the lad was in despair. Then, wondering what he should do, he clasped his hands and in so doing happened to rub the brass ring.

To his amazement, there came a blind-ing flash of light and a huge genie appeared. "What is your command, master?" he asked.

There was a flash of light and great clouds of green and red and blue smoke swirled around the room as another huge genie appeared.

"I am the genie of the lamp and your wish is my command," he said.

"Astounding!" exclaimed Aladdin. "First one genie and now another."

His mother fearfully covered her eyes. What magic was this?

Now, after all his adventures, Aladdin was hungry.

"Bring us a meal, please," he said. And

Well, as you can imagine, the thing that Aladdin wanted most of all was to go home to his mother.

But first, he picked up the old lamp and then he picked some of the fruit from the pretty garden. The fruit was so bright and shiny that Aladdin was sure his mother would like it.

Then Aladdin turned to the genie of the ring.

"Take me home, please," he said.

POUF!

In a flash, Aladdin was home with his mother.

How surprised she was to see him and Aladdin had to explain about how his uncle had shut him in the underground garden and how he had escaped with the help of the genie of the ring.

What a strange affair!

Aladdin's mother picked up the old lamp. "What a dirty thing," she said and gave it a rub. GOODNESS!

at once the genie brought a wonderful meal on golden dishes standing on a gold tray. It was all a little frightening.

Aladdin's mother began to feel quite upset.

"All this magic and flashing lights and genies popping up is just too much for me," she gasped. "It isn't right for plain folk like us, Aladdin. Don't rub the ring or the magic lamp again."

So Aladdin, who liked to please his mother, put the lamp away in a drawer and didn't touch it for years.

And in actual fact there was no need. Whenever Aladdin or his mother needed any money, they just sold one of the gold dishes on which the genie had brought their magic meal—and when the dishes were gone, they sold the gold tray, and when all the gold was gone, they started to sell some of the bright fruit that Aladdin had brought back from the secret underground garden. For it turned out that the fruits were precious jewels.

Now all this money lasted for years and years and Aladdin was a grown-up young man before even a quarter of the fruit—or jewels, as they actually were—had been sold.

How happy life was.

But then—alas and alack!

Something happened to disturb all that calm happy life and in a moment Aladdin and his mother were plunged back into worry and adventure.

One day, as Aladdin was walking through the town, he heard a lot of shouting and banging of drums and clattering of feet.

Everyone fell back in fear to make way and striding proudly down the centre of the road came a procession from the royal palace. And carried in the centre of the procession, seated in a beautiful golden chair, was the king's daughter, Princess Badroul.

Aladdin fell in love with her at once.

Oh, what a shame!

For how could Aladdin's love lead to anything but unhappiness?

Kings' daughters do not marry the sons of poor tailors.

By no means!

But Aladdin's mind was made up.

He went home and told his mother he was going to marry the king's daughter.

"Oh, Aladdin, Aladdin!" gasped his mother. "What foolish idea is this! You will never be allowed to marry the king's daughter. Why, the king will cut off our heads at the very idea."

But as it happened, for once Aladdin's mother was wrong.

The king was a man greedy for wealth, as Aladdin knew well, and Aladdin sent his mother to the palace to show the king the fruit jewels from the secret garden.

The king's tiny eyes shone.

"Tell your son that if he sends me forty trays of jewels, as good as the jewels you are showing me, together with twenty Greek slaves and twenty African slaves, and if he builds a palace next to my own, but much more splendid—oh, and it must be finished all in one day—if he does all that, then he may marry my daughter."

It all seemed terribly difficult to Aladdin's mother, but of course with the help of the magic lamp, which Aladdin took from its drawer, all the difficult tasks were accomplished with no trouble.

And then dressed in magnificent clothes

and riding a white horse, followed by a procession of the slaves carrying the jewels and his mother riding in a palanquin, Aladdin went to the palace to claim the hand of the princess.

Of course in his wonderful new clothes Aladdin looked very important and as soon as he arrived at the palace he was shown in to see the king.

"I have brought the forty trays of jewels carried by the twenty Greek slaves and the twenty African slaves, your majesty," bowed Aladdin.

The king was amazed, because he had not really believed that anyone could do the things he had asked Aladdin to do. However, he looked at all the jewels and the slaves and he was very pleased.

"You seem like just the sort of son-in-law I have been looking for," he smiled.

Then he remembered he had asked for a magnificent palace to be built next door.

"But what about that palace, eh?" he smiled, quite sure that Aladdin could

never have built a palace in a day.

"Look over your shoulder, your majesty," replied Aladdin.

The king looked.

AMAZING!

Next to his own palace the king saw a fantastic building, more marvellous than anything he had ever seen before in his life.

"I can see that you will be a really useful sort of chap to have about the place," beamed the king. "You may marry my daughter at once."

So the king sent for his daughter Princess Badroul.

"You are to marry Aladdin," instructed the king.

Luckily Princess Badroul fell in love with Aladdin at first sight, or things could have been rather difficult, but they did get married and they lived very happily for quite a long time—but not for ever after.

Unfortunately there was still trouble in store for poor Aladdin, who had never done a day's harm to anyone. But great wealth often brings great trouble.

Now, you may have been wondering what happened to the wicked magician after he slammed the door on Aladdin and, as he thought, locked Aladdin in the secret underground garden for ever.

Well, the magician had been quite happy for years doing bad deeds and thinking how miserable Aladdin must be in the secret garden and serve him jolly well right, he thought.

But the day came when the magician thought he would like to make another attempt at obtaining the magic lamp and then when he started making a few enquiries he learned of Aladdin's escape and present good fortune.

He was furious!

At once he thought of a plan to get the magic lamp for himself.

Disguised as a pedlar, he took a basket of lamps all shiny and new and stood outside Aladdin's palace calling:

"New lamps for old. New lamps for old."

Now by ill chance a servant girl heard him. And by even worse chance it happened to be a girl who had seen the magic lamp in Aladdin's room.

At once she exchanged the old magic lamp for a new lamp.

"How clever I am," she smiled—but oh—what trouble she was making.

As soon as the magician had the lamp in his hands, he rubbed it and summoned the genie.

"Your wish is my command, O master," bowed the genie.

"Yes, yes, all right, don't waste time chatting," snapped the magician. "I want you to magic Aladdin's palace and the princess and all the riches and servants with me to the desert of Morocco."

Pouf!

There was a blinding flash of light and Aladdin's lovely palace disappeared with everything in it.

As it happened, Aladdin was out riding at the time. At once the king had him seized and thrown into prison.

Poor Aladdin! What could he do!

You see, the king was furious that his daughter had disappeared.

"I want my daughter back, you rascal," he shouted at Aladdin, "and I shouldn't be sorry to see the palace back either, for it was worth a lot of money. I know you can do magic tricks—after all you built the palace in a day. So get my daughter and the palace back or you stay in prison for ever."

How unfair!

Never mind! There was one good thing about the whole sorry business. Aladdin was still wearing the magic ring the magician had given him years ago and which he had used to get himself out of the secret underground garden.

Aladdin pulled himself together and rubbed the magic ring.

At once the genie of the ring appeared. "Your wish is my command," he bowed.

"Thank goodness the magic of the ring is still working," smiled Aladdin.

Then he asked the genie to take him to the princess, his wife. In a flash—Aladdin was in Morocco.

When the magic smoke cleared, Aladdin found himself standing in the princess's bedroom.

"Thank goodness you are here," she gasped. "The wicked magician is trying to make me marry him and tonight there is to be a wedding feast."

At once Aladdin thought of a plan. That evening at the feast he hid behind the magician's chair and slipped a sleeping powder into his wine. When the magician slept, Aladdin took back the lamp from the magician's pocket—and then of course Aladdin's troubles were over. He called up the genie and ordered himself, the princess and the palace and everything in it—except the magician—to be taken back to their proper home.

So then of course Aladdin and the princess and the king and Aladdin's mother were all very happy.

And as Aladdin took good care of the lamp from then on, they lived happily ever after.

As for the poor old wicked magician, he woke up cold and alone in the desert of Morocco and decided not to bother with lamps any more. HOORAY!

The Shepherd Paul

Once upon a time, when a shepherd was taking his flock out to pasture, he found a baby lying in the meadow.

How the baby came to be there, no one ever knew, but the kind shepherd looked after the poor little thing and brought it up as his own.

Now the years went by and when the baby, which had been called Paul, was almost grown to be a man, he decided that he would like to go out into the great, big world and seek his fortune—and perhaps even find his parents.

"You have been kind to me, foster father," he said to the shepherd, "but I do not wish to be a shepherd all my life."

So the shepherd lent Paul a horse and they said goodbye and off Paul rode.

Now, there was one very unusual thing about Paul, apart from the fact that he had been found in a field, that is. Paul was very strong—VERY strong. He was *amazingly* strong.

Why, even as a lad he could tear trees up by their roots and when it came to wrestling, Paul could beat anyone he had ever met.

Now, as he went on his journey, Paul met, one after the other, three strong men,

who all liked wrestling. One after the other young Paul beat the three men at wrestling and they all became friends and travelled together. Or Paul thought they were friends. He was to find out differently.

One night, as the four friends were cooking supper round their camp fire, a dwarf came and tried to steal their food, but Shepherd Paul caught him and tied him to a tree.

However, the next morning the dwarf was gone and so was the tree. The dwarf had pulled it up at the roots and then escaped down a huge hole in the ground, dragging the tree with him.

This all seemed rather strange and frightening and the three men wanted to go on their way, but Shepherd Paul said he would go down the hole. Perhaps he would find his fortune there.

So the three men lowered Paul down the hole in a basket and then sat and waited for him to come back.

When he reached the bottom of the hole, Paul found himself in a sunlit land with a fine castle standing in a nearby meadow.

Shepherd Paul walked over and knocked at the door of the castle. A beautiful maiden answered the door.

"Go away," she gasped. "A fierce dragon lives here and he will kill you if he sees you."

But Shepherd Paul was so strong that dragons did not bother him. He slew the dragon without getting out of breath.

Then the beautiful maiden told Paul that the dragon was the dwarf in disguise and that he had kidnapped her from her home in the world above. Waiting only to take all the treasure from the castle, Paul took the maiden back to the hole and called to his friends to pull them up.

"Climb into the basket," they called.

But when Shepherd Paul and the maiden and the treasure reached the top of the hole, the three so-called friends grabbed the maiden and the treasure and then let go the rope so that Shepherd Paul and the basket fell back into the earth.

Then the three men ran off, thinking that they would never see Paul again.

But they were wrong. A little fawn had seen what had happened and the fawn fetched Paul's horse and between the two of them they hauled Paul back up the hole.

Paul raced after his faithless friends and when they saw him, they left the maiden and the treasure and ran off and never came back again.

And Paul and the maiden and the horse and fawn and, of course, the treasure went back to the old shepherd and they all lived happily ever after.